Danny
AND THE
DreamWeaver

BY

Published ℗ 2016 DV Books, an imprint of Digital Vista, Inc.
Copyright © 2015 Rich DiSilvio (aka Mark Poe)

Printed in the USA. *First printing.*

Cover art, character conceptions & illustrations, and interior book layout by © Rich DiSilvio. Any photographs or other images are from purchased collections, Rich DiSilvio's photo library or courtesy of Wikipedia's public domain images.

CATALOGING-IN-PUBLICATION DATA

Names: DiSilvio, Rich.
Title: Danny and the Dreamweaver / Mark Poe
Description: New York, USA: DV Books, an imprint of Digital Vista, Inc., 2016.
Identifiers: ISBN **978-0-9976807-3-7** (paperback) |
ISBN **978-0-9976807-4-4** (ebook)
Subjects: LC: Fantasy. | Time travel--Fiction. | Artists--Fiction.

DANNY AND THE *DreamWeaver*

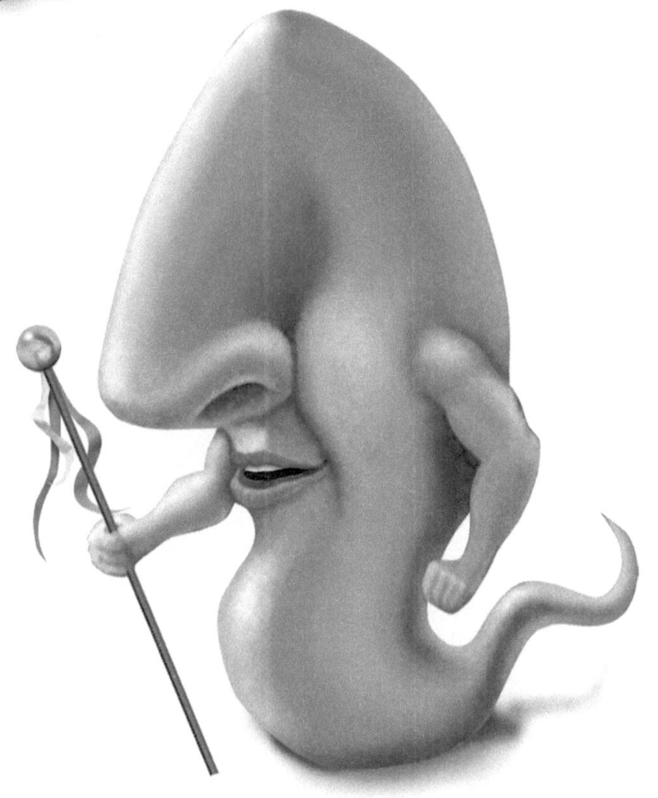

BY MARK POE

Chapter 1

$\mathcal{D}$anny looked up at the clock out of the corner of his eye as his ninth-grade art teacher babbled on and on about some dead old artists from the past. It was the last period of the day at Seacrest Middle School, and his leg bounced impatiently while he waited to hear the bell ring—the bell of *freedom!*

He veered back at Ms. Minnts and rolled his eyes. Sure, he thought Ms. Minnts was sweet enough, and even sort of cute for an old lady of thirty-three, but why did he need to learn about this stuff? His Xbox 360 and PlayStation games blew this stagnant old dribble away big time! So too did killer CG movies, like *The Avengers* or *Transformers.*

Come on, Mz. Mintzmeat! Danny's mind carped. *Hurry up! I have two real tests I have to study for tomorrow, and I just wanna get home, eat a banana and peanut butter sandwich, and play Bloodborne. I mean crack open my science book and possibly my English lit book, too. Yeah, more boring stuff all right, but at least they might be somewhat useful. After all, science is what made video games and my iPhone possible. And I know ideas for video games and movies come from authors, so I guess literature can be sort of tolerable, but—*

The bell let out its glorious last ring!

Ah! Salvation! Danny thought as he and his classmates began scooping up their books and shoving them in their backpacks. His fellow students started scurrying out the door, yet Danny was still half-zoning and fumbling with his pencils. However, he was keen to notice Johnny Dolan dash out the door. Danny huffed.

Johnny Dolan happens to be Danny's next-door neighbor, or perhaps *archenemy* would be a better word. Whether it was competing in class, on the soccer field, or racing down the path to Jones Beach on their bikes, Johnny and Danny have been battling each other since they were tykes on trikes. A little spat had turned into a fistfight when they were six, and they had never gotten over it.

Shoot! Danny snarled as he made a beeline for the door, making sure not to make eye contact with Mz. Mintzmeat.

But just as he reached the door, Ms. Minnts harkened, "Danny Venuti! Come back here."

Danny's Nikes made a screeching sound as he skid to a stop. He rolled his eyes as he spun his head around. "Ms. Minnts, I have a lot of studying to do for tomorrow. I have—"

"Come here, I said," she commanded. "This will only take a minute."

Irritably, Danny quickly sneaked a peek out the door, only to see Johnny hopping on his bike and tearing out with a snide grin on his freckled face. With a cringe and a hiss, Danny pivoted about and shuffled slowly toward her desk, while his fellow students passed him by with stifled smiles on their faces as they exited.

Standing in front of Ms. Minnts's desk, Danny muttered, "What is it?"

Ms. Minnts always had to struggle to be domineering and her somewhat commanding face morphed back to her normal gentle smile. Closing the large art book on her desk, she gazed up. "Danny, I noticed you were daydreaming and looking at the clock again. You really must pay attention if you plan on learning anything and passing this class."

Danny just stared at her with glass doll eyes, his mind already slipping into a coma. He hated these same old boring lectures, and would have preferred having his teeth yanked out of his head, like in Grand Theft Auto, as she droned on, "I can see by that cold expression on your adorable face that art is not something that interests you, but—"

Danny awoke from his coma upon hearing the words "adorable face." With his attention snagged and his face now blushing, he interjected, "Yeah, I'm sorry, Ms. Minnts. You're a swell teacher and all, but I really don't see the need to learn this stuff. It's just a stupid elective, and I have some *real* classes that I need to study for. Science and English are really—"

"Important, I know," she interrupted. "But so too is art, because even electives have an important role to play in your life."

Danny snickered with an irreverent snort, sounding like a pig. "Yeah, sure they do."

"Danny, your life should not be focused on only one or two things. That's why we offer a liberal arts program in your early years. Sure, most students will need to decide on a major upon entering college, but being well rounded is critical for everyone. Do you realize that nowadays many people lose their jobs and need to find work in different fields?"

As Danny's eyes rolled, Ms. Minnts realized she was losing his interest once again and changed course. "I know you're too young to appreciate that, but think of it this way; tell me who *you* admire, and I don't mean family members. I mean someone famous who inspires you."

Without hesitation, Danny blurted, "Steve Jobs!" Becoming animated, he added, "He made Apple computers, started Pixar, and invented the iPod, iPad, and iPhone. Better yet, he quit college. So how important is school anyhow?"

Ms. Minnts chuckled. "Okay, I can see how you think school is a waste of time. Even Pink Floyd chanted, 'We don't need no education,' while Alice Cooper loved when 'school's out for summer.' But without having a high school education Jobs wouldn't have been able to communicate too well (not having learned proper English), let alone known much else to form a foundation to build his future on. As I demonstrated in class yesterday, during my lecture on famous architects, Frank Lloyd Wright could never have built any of his fabulous buildings without a solid foundation. And figuratively speaking, the same holds true for everyone else, regardless of what field of interest they engage in. And Steve Jobs would never have had an interest in computers if he hadn't learned about all the primitive computers before him or the pioneers who built them. Ideas cannot be hatched in a vacuum, Danny."

Danny quasi nodded, quasi agreeing, but glanced up at the clock. It was 3:40 PM. There was no way to beat Johnny home now, or even catch up to him. His shoulders drooped as he looked back at his teacher. "Yeah, I guess I know what you're trying to say. But I have no interest in art or architecture, unless it's the architecture and artwork of a video game." As Ms. Minnts listened attentively, Danny continued, "At least that would be cool. You know, to create a new an exciting environment, something with action and a cool fantasy-like setting. But that requires science and technology, Ms. Minnts, not learning about Van Gogh's chopped-off ear or Whistler's ugly old mother sitting in a stupid chair."

Ms. Minnts giggled. "Well, I'm glad you listened to *some* of my lectures and have a passion for something. But developing video games requires more than just science and technology, Danny. It takes imagination, and some of the most creative minds in history happened to have been artists and authors. And they, in turn, have inspired people with other interests to do amazing things in their particular fields."

Danny's smirk clearly telegraphed his doubt as Ms. Minnts paused, searched her memory, then continued, "For example, the song *I Am the Walrus* by The Beatles was inspired by Lewis Carroll's poem *The Walrus and the Carpenter*. And many artists and musicians have made paintings or songs about scenes in Dante's literary masterpiece, *The Divine Comedy*. And what most people don't realize, Danny, is that artists design the world we live in…" As Danny rolled his eyes, she continued, "from the clothes we wear to the cars and bikes we drive to the houses we live in to the bridges we cross to the advertisements that flood our mailboxes and TV screens to the intricate parts of every machine, they are all designed by artists of some sort, and they all seek ideas from those around us or from people in our past. And sometimes they get ideas subconsciously, without realizing it. So you see, inspiration often times comes from the least likely of places."

Danny pondered her words for a moment, as his eyes connected with the Apple logo on her laptop. "Yeah, in fact I heard some stories about what that Apple logo symbolizes, you know, with that bite mark in it. One story said it represented the bite Eve took from the apple that Satan gave her in the Garden of Eden. Supposedly her curiosity represents Apple's curiosity to learn new things. So I guess old stories can be kinda useful."

Ms. Minnts spun her laptop around. Her screen saver was simply a floating text quote with a photo of its author. Danny's eyes widened, surprised that the photo was not of a famous artist or architect. She said, "Never forget what Albert Einstein said, Danny. *Imagination is more important than knowledge.*"

Danny was flabbergasted, and not only for her choice of a screen saver as he snickered. "Geez, I know Einstein was a mega genius, Ms. Minnts, but that quote is just stupid."

Ms. Minnts stifled a chuckle. "Well, Danny, when I first read it, I also thought it must have been a joke or a mistake, but it does make perfect sense."

Danny scratched his chin. "Seriously?"

Ms. Minnts rose from her desk. "Most certainly. Because knowledge only pertains to things we have learned about up until now. Yet it takes imagination to think creatively to unravel the mysteries of our world, and in that way spawn new ideas to expand our knowledge. So you see, artists and authors have always been at the forefront of creativity, along with scientists and inventors who engage their imaginations. And that's why I wished you were paying attention to my lecture today about some truly great artists."

Danny shrugged his shoulders, aloof, yet certainly preferring to be knowledgeable rather than imaginative, as he gave his standard reply, "Well, I guess I'll try harder, Ms. Minnts. But I really must get going. I have—"

"Yes, yes, I know, Danny," Ms. Minnts interjected. "Run along. But you *will* be tested on this material on Friday. So I strongly suggest you open a book or two, or borrow a friend's notes. Got it?"

"Yep, got it!" Danny said, as he made an about face and bolted out the door.

Running outside to the bike rack, Danny unlocked his new Diamondback Podium 16-speed bike, which he received last week for his birthday, and hopped on.

Johnny Dolan had always ribbed Danny for the old beat-up piece of rust and rubber he had previously, being that it was a hand-me-down from his dad. The Huffy Strider 10-speed road bike may have been cool in its day, back when the dinosaurs roamed the streets in 1979, but it received a great deal of ridicule from Johnny, who had laughed at its heavy, rusted steel frame, which made the Huffy seem like an old WWII Sherman tank compared to the new lightweight aluminum frames of today, which soar like F-117 stealth fighters.

Danny grasped the handlebars and began pedaling. Zipping past a crew of street workers hacking away with pickaxes behind a series of orange cones, Danny weaved in and out of the last four cones, as the construction workers shook their heads—one yelling, "Hey, kid! Be careful!" With the wind in his hair and the straps of his backpack flapping wildly in his wake, Danny pumped and pedaled, eager to get home.

Turning a sharp corner, his eyes caught a glimpse of a colorful new poster for the Bronx Zoo. It was hanging on the wall of the Seacrest train station as he cruised past. He was about to stop, when, to his surprise, he saw Johnny up ahead, crouched over, and fiddling with his bike. He had a flat tire! Danny's face beamed as he sped past him, and jeered, "Too bad, *Loser!*" Danny cruised several more blocks, then zoomed up his driveway and dismounted.

"Ha! I beat Johnny Rocket home after all," Danny mumbled with glee. Then he opened the garage door and hung his bike on the wall rack.

Running into the house, he tossed his backpack on the couch, and headed straight for the kitchen. He looked at the clock: 4:20. He had two hours to eat and hit the couch for a nap. *Ah, plenty of time,* he thought, as he made his banana and peanut butter sandwich, poured a large glass of milk, and then plopped on the sofa.

He took a few bites, gulped down some milk, and picked up his iPad. Surfing a few websites, he stopped briefly to read the upcoming news about Quantum Break for Xbox 360, a video game whose players can manipulate time, then fired up Candy Crush, opting to play a silly and less taxing game to ease his weary mind.

Danny slid the candy puzzle pieces with his index finger while his eyelids grew heavier and heavier. Sinking deeper into the couch, Danny leaned over, his head resting on his backpack, as his finger eventually slid off the screen, falling limp by his side. Dozing off into a deep slumber, Danny's mind drifted into a black void.

All was silent, until, in the recesses of his mind, a small blurry image began to appear. Slowly, the image grew, lighting up the darkness in his mind, as if the opening fade-in of a movie. A sprinkled array of stars and planets, looking almost like candies, floated toward him, then faded as they drifted slowly past.

Out of this stellar mist appeared what seemed to be an old city, with horse drawn carriages and shadowy figures walking the streets, some in top hats others wearing berets. In the distance, a large steel structure dominated the surreal landscape, looking like what appeared to be the Eifel Tower. Yet that vision faded quickly, morphing into a fanciful interior of a room, decorated with elaborate moldings, tapestries on the wall, and old-styled furniture, all bathed in a swirling mist.

Emerging out this mysterious haze appeared an odd-looking creature, unlike anything Danny had ever seen before. Despite its strange appearance, it was neither frightful nor intimidating. In fact, it was rather comical looking with a huge nose and a welcoming smile. Standing in the midst of this room, and holding a staff, the strange-looking figure spoke!

Chapter 2

"Greetings, Danny. Oh, yes, and please be advised that you are here in spirit only. You have no physical presence in this place."

"Hold on!" Danny's voice sounded, like a voice over in a movie. "This is *my* dream. How come I'm not in it?"

"Because this is my domain, Danny. I'm the dreamweaver. As you'll see, I even hold the eminent role of narrator and main character in this fantastical world. You, my friend, are just a dreaming spectator, so you might as well relax and listen. Or you can choose to daydream, like you normally do. But I have a fascinating tale to tell, whether you listen or not."

"This is stupid!" Danny's voice radiated with annoyance. "You're in *my* head, so *I* make the rules. In fact, I can simply think of a new character that will zap your butt right out of my head. And POW! You'll be toast."

"Aw, there's so much violence in your tone, Danny. It truly is a reflection of those crazy video games you play. Those killer tactics have no place here, Danny. Besides, as you should know by now, people cannot dictate their dreams. Dreams have a life and will of their own. Haven't you realized that?"

"Well, I guess, I suppose so. Yeah."

"So please, relax. This is not a combative video game that relies on shooting and killing people. No, no, this dream is far above such base actions and savage behaviors. I would like to take you on a different kind of adventure, one filled with a little mystery and suspense, a touch of humor, and perhaps even educational in some way. But I guarantee it *will* be imaginative."

"Well, I can tell that already by how weird you look," Danny said, "especially with that big nose. So who the heck are you anyhow?"

"My name is Nostrildamus. And as you'll see, I have a nose for sniffing out prophecies, just like a bloodhound seeking a smelly warthog with a bad case of gas."

Danny's laugh echoed off the walls of *my* French-styled living room (Yes, I told you I would narrate), which had nicely solidified, the dream world now seeming ever so real.

"Well, allow me to clarify, Danny. It's not so much smell. I can *see* into the future."

Again Danny laughed, seeing that I had no eyes.

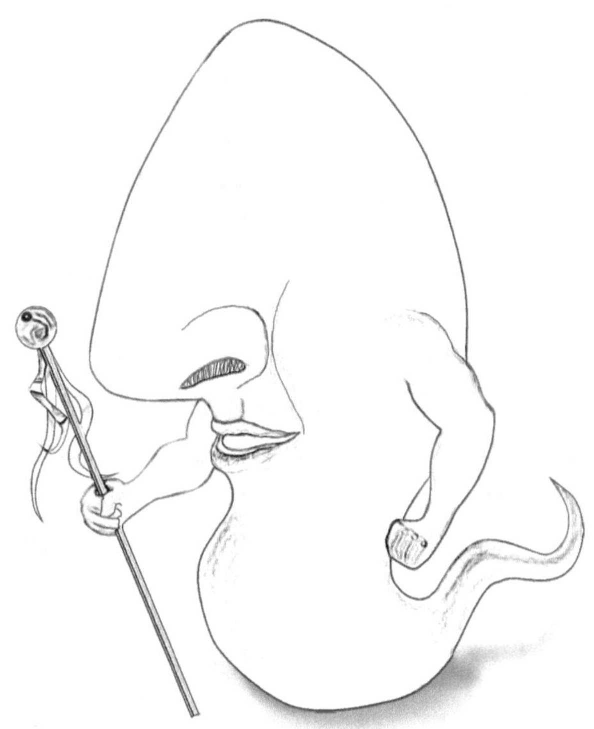

"Better yet," I continued, "I can even travel to these amazing places."

"How so?" he asked, clearly doubting every word I said.

"Well, I'm also a bit of an inventor, Danny. But I must admit; my time travel machine was not very good. To put it bluntly, it sucked bananas! Just like the ones on your sandwich."

Again Danny chuckled. As you can see, I can be quite capricious at times.

"You see, Danny, I had a vision about a man who invented a time machine; I mean a really nifty one. His name was O.G. Swells. And Oh God was his time machine really swell. So much so, that I just had to make my own machine to visit this crafty fellow."

"Hmm, that name sounds kind of familiar," Danny said. "But I'm really into games and movies about time travel, Nostrildamus. So this *might* be interesting."

"I hope so, so listen up. Fortunately, my time travel machine managed to get me there, but it broke down the moment it crash-landed in England in 1895. That's where and when this old geezer lived. And as I found out later, Swells was a swell author. Perhaps you've heard of his stories, like *The Invisible Man* or *War of the Worlds*? He even wrote a book called *The Time Machine.*"

"Heck yeah, I saw *War of the Worlds!*" Danny replied excitedly. "It was a wicked movie with Tom Cruise and Dakota Fanning. She was pretty hot, but that flick had some awesome special effects, too. Yet I didn't see those other ones."

"Well, although those stories were all made into movies, Danny, I'm referring to the original novels. You know, *books!*...those things with two covers and pages in between…those *boring* things you hate to crack open."

"Yeah, Nosy. I know what you mean. You don't mind me calling you *Nosy*, do you?"

"Snot at all," I said with a snort.

As Danny chuckled, I continued…

"Well, getting back to my tale, after I crash-landed into O.G. Swells's house, I—oh yes, did I forget to mention that? Well, uh, yes, yes, I did, and I must say, he was very surprised to see me. And not just for the ghastly damage I had done to his lovely abode. You see, he had read about me, being that I've managed to carve a nice little name for myself in the history books. Not that I'd expect you to know that, Danny, but I must say, Swells didn't expect to see what he saw."

"I can understand *that*," Danny said with a chuckle.

"Yes indeed. As you can see, I'm a humungous nose with a serpent-like body, two arms, extremely handsome, well, okay, perhaps just cute…and naturally I'm green. And I don't mean green as in being a rookie, Danny. No, no, I am far from that. I mean my skin color is green. At least it is to anyone who is not colorblind. And even though I do have a green thumb, I must admit, I'm not very good at gardening."

As Danny giggled, I continued, "However, O.G. Swells biggest shock was that I have no eyes. Granted, that does seem to baffle most people, since I do *see* into the future and the past."

"Yeah," Danny blurted, "that *is* really odd, just like this dream."

"Yes, indeed it is," I replied with a chuckle. "At any rate, Swells and I hit it off rather well, and boy oh boy did we have a dandy ol' time. Swells took me on several trips with his time machine to visit famous people, and I must say, it not only worked like a charm, but it also looked really, really sharp, like a Batmobile or something. You know, with wild wing-like fins, bubble glass, and a bunch of crazy gizmos inside. Every place we visited, people turned and looked, then begged us for a ride."

"Okay, now you're talkin'!" Danny blurted. "Let's see this time machine."

"In *time*, Danny, in *time!*" I replied with a touch of wit. "But you see, after a while, Swells had gotten so tired of being harassed, that he threw up his hands and declared, 'I've had enough! I have other things to do. The time machine is yours, Nostrildamus.'

"I was quite shocked and elated, as you can imagine. That's also one of the great things about travelling through time, you get to meet all these fantastic people, and even get some nifty gifts. But don't get me wrong; O.G. Swells didn't just give me his time machine for no good reason, Danny. I had helped him with his research. My visions proved quite useful to him while he wrote his amazing books."

I slithered over to my *caquetoire* and sat down, and then…oh, yes, a *caquetoire* is simply a fancy name for a French Renaissance chair. After all, I *am* French, and *was* born during the Renaissance. Anyhow, I continued, "In fact, Danny, those alien space ships in his *War of the Worlds* novel came from, yes, none other than yours truly."

"Hmm," Danny said. "Just today, Ms. Minnts told me how people get inspiration from the least likely of places. So I was wondering where Swells got his spacey ideas. But if he had a time machine, why didn't he just go into the future to search for ideas himself?"

"Excellent point, Danny. But you see, Swells had complained about some crazy Y2K computer glitch that prevented his machine from going past the year 2000. So my visions of the distant future (the year 3025 to be exact) had given me some amazing ideas about space ships, which I later relayed to him."

Danny's voice rose with excitement, "*Now* this is starting to get really interesting, Nosy! So are we gonna explore some distant planet to fight some ugly-ass aliens who wanna destroy Earth?"

I chuckled. "Danny, as I told you, all that shooting and killing nonsense you do on Xbox is not what this dream is about. The tale I wish to impart is about my fantastic journeys into the past and future when I met some very interesting artists."

"Oh, geez! I knew this dream was gonna turn wimpy somehow. Are you sure you're not in the wrong kid's head? This is stupid!"

"Now, now, don't be so negative, Danny. I know you're not thrilled about art and the magnificent people who create it, but I guarantee, you *will* find this interesting."

"Whatever," Danny moaned glumly. "Go on," he said, almost in protest.

"Very well. This all occurred two months ago, when I had a startling vision. I was in the kitchen eating a ham sandwich, when I shrieked, 'I see! I see! Oh say can I see…' And, no, not *by the dawn's early light*, Danny, but rather I saw a disturbed little fellow, lemon yellow. And—"

"The man was yellow?"

"No, no. *He* was not yellow. *He* was red, cherry red. It's the splashes of paint I had seen that were yellow, and many other colors, too. It was a terrible mess. Then the chap's face came back into view, but the vision was fuzzy, so I couldn't make out whom it is. One thing was for sure, however, this fellow was very upset, and I wanted to offer him my assistance. That's when I knew it was time for another trip!"

Chapter 3

"Next, I had to concentrate on dates. Not the ones we're told to memorize in school, or the ones on the calendar, because the only important dates for me are the ones that flash in my mind. You see, that's how I zero-in on the people in my visions. And *bingo!* The number 1512 appeared. And the place was Rome, Italy.

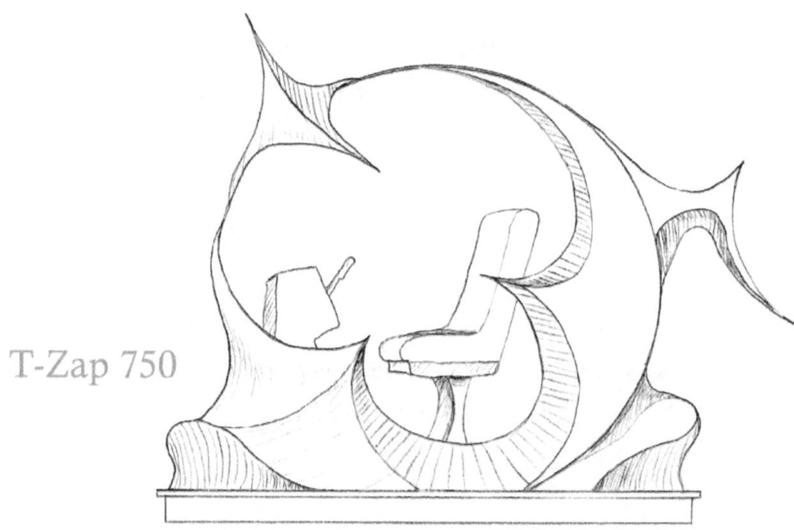

"I then strapped myself into the T-Zap 750, or Time Zapper, and programmed those settings. If you're wondering what the 750 stands for, it means absolutely nothing. I just thought it sounded cool. We'll drop that."

"Yeah, I'm pretty sucky at math and numbers, Nosy, so axe that. But I'm glad I finally got to see this machine of yours. At least *one* thing in this boring tale will be killer."

"Actually, the story truly starts from here, Danny. Therefore, I'll be switching into full narrator mode henceforth, so I suggest you get your make-believe popcorn and soda, and strap yourself in for the ride."

With everything set, I pulled the lever, and I was *oooooffffffffffffff!*"

Static-electric webs of lightning snapped while steam billowed out of the T-Zap. Its chrome gyro rings spun wildly and everything had become blurry, my surroundings vanishing into a fluffy white cloud. The dials on the T-Zap spun rapidly like the propellers on fighter planes I had seen during my visits to the first two World Wars. But I wasn't traveling that far ahead in time; this trip would be over in—

BANG! BELCH! BOOM! BURP! Sssssssssss.

I peered down at the monitor. It read 1512 and the map indicated that I had landed in an alley near the Via Veneto, a street in the heart of Rome. And no crash-landing into a building, either. "Perfect!" Or perhaps I should have said *"Perfetto!"*

But I soon realized I had company. Three Italians had spotted me and began running toward me. Quickly, I grabbed my trusty staff, and prepared to make the T-Zap invisible. Lucky for me, I invented a cloaking device while reading O.G. Swells book *The Invisible Man*. It's amazing how great ideas pop into your head when studying the works of other people. It pays to read.

Danny grunted—perhaps not appreciating my not-so-subtle hint, or maybe he was busy noshing on that make-believe popcorn.

Anyhow, then came the fun part, you know, watching people's baffled faces when the T-Zap disappeared. I flipped the switch on my staff, and zap! Gone! As the three Italian men came to an abrupt halt, one said, "Hey, *signore* (That means *mister* in Italian), where did your strange metal wagon go?"

Meanwhile, his two buddies asked the same question, all with the same silly look on their faces.

It was time to play dumb, a role I enjoy. "What wagon?" I said, as I spun around to view nothing. Well, not nothing, there were buildings behind me, and a cobble-stoned street, but you get the idea.

Danny's voice interrupted. "Yeah, yeah, I get the idea," he moaned. "Go on, Nosy, let's get this over with."

"Very well," I replied. So then the man's lips twisted with annoyance, as he said, "Are you trying to make fools of us?"

"Perish the thought," I said. Actually I lied. "But as you can see, I'm as blind as a bat. I have no eyes." That always seems to flummox people. Even my close friends, or the King and Queen of France, whom I humbly serve, still can't understand how a blind person can see into the future or the past. Actually, it puzzles me, too. But sometimes disabilities come with miraculous perks.

Anyhow, the Italian man was *not* satisfied, as he snapped, "Well, we all saw a big, bright flash!" Heatedly, he placed his hands on his hips and growled, "You may have no eyes, *signore* Rattle Snake, but *we* do!"

Some people seem to mistake me for a reptile, so I've learned to overlook such silly remarks. "Well, perhaps it was my staff," I said as I lifted it and cunningly reflected the sun off its metallic ball right into their eyes. The three men squinted and scratched their heads, confused. Meanwhile, I shrewdly changed topics. "I'm looking for a red fellow, about this height." I extended my hand straight out. "And he appears to be a painter, an artist, if you will."

Now distracted, they eagerly offered up the information and directed me to a place called the Sistine Chapel. It's located in the Vatican, the home of the Roman Catholic Church and the pope.

As I strolled along the streets of Rome with the aid of my staff, tapping the street so I could *hear* my surroundings, I sensed the attractive buildings, ancient ruins, and the rumble of people shopping and drinking espresso. That's when I had to stop and have a cup of cappuccino; the smell of that deep, rich Italian coffee was just too enticing.

Stopping at Milo's café, I also had two cannolis, three biscotti, and four tri-colored Rainbow cookies. I love food! And not just desserts. In my mind I gaped at the succulent meats and vegetables in the display case and the dried sausages and provolone hanging from the ceiling. The smells tickled my large, sensitive nose and my mouth began watering. I wanted desperately to eat a big meaty sandwich, but I had to get moving along.

Resuming my journey, I slithered down the street, tapping the ground with my staff and focusing on the visions in my head. Weaving through crowds of people, all dressed in their colorful Renaissance clothing, I crossed a bridge over the Tiber River and finally arrived at the Vatican. A huge colonnade, in the shape of two half circles, formed a welcoming entrance to the towering Saint Peter's Basilica, which sat majestically before me. Eagerly, I slithered into the immense basilica, when a cardinal, not the bird, the human kind, stopped me. Being that he was dressed in red, I figured he was a friend of the red artist I was seeking.

But evidently, he had something else on his mind, as he growled, "How dare you slither into our sacred Holy Church! Away with you, Lucifer!"

I choked! "My name is *not* Lucifer," I said, "it is Nostrildamus." I could sense the cardinal eyeing me up as he pulled out a gold crucifix from his pocket and shoved it toward my face. "Sure you are, and my name is Judas Iscariot."

I recoiled. "Is it really? Dear Lord! Are you a time traveler, too? You're way out of your time period, Judas."

The cardinal huffed and rolled his eyes. "Of course I'm not Judas, you blind fool! That was just an expression, a sarcastic remark. In other words, your claim of *not* being Lucifer (the evil snake who rules in Hell) is just as preposterous as *me* claiming to be Judas (the sinful apostle that betrayed Christ.)"

"Oh, dear. Now I see. You think I'm the Devil, the serpent that slithered into the Garden of Eden and tricked mankind." I waved my finger. "No, no! I assure you, that is *not* me."

The cardinal moaned as he grasped a large brass candleholder and thrust the flaming end toward my face. "You cannot fool me, Lucifer! I know the Devil is a trickster. You may have fooled Eve into biting the apple, but you won't trick me with your bogus bait! So what evil intent do you have in mind? Tell me, you big, green, lying, evil, slimy snake?"

I just had to chuckle. "No need to use all those adjectives, Cardinal." After all, he *did* go a bit overboard. "I have no evil intent in mind," I continued, "I came here in search of a man, much like you, being that he is also red and working within these sacred walls. He is an artist. And I was told he is working on a massive painting, which you call a fresco, on the ceiling of your Sistine Chapel."

The cardinal lowered the flaming candle, and sized me up from head to tail. "What business do you have with this artist—to pose as the snake for his rendition of the *Expulsion from Eden*?"

This birdbrain just didn't give up! Perhaps this cardinal *was* part bird. Irritated, I shook my head. "No, no. You must believe me, *Judas*." Yes, I *can* be a little devil. ☺

The cardinal grew even redder as he flew out of his cage into a rage. "I told you, I am NOT Judas, you moron!"

"Well, you never did mention your name," I said. "But as I told you, I am here because I saw that this artist is very upset. Something is very wrong. I also saw lots of colors, but my vision was quite hazy. So I'm here to offer my assistance."

The cardinal snickered. "You *saw* him and lots of colors? Ha! How can a snake with no eyes see anything, unless it is the Devil himself? Surrender or leave the premises! You will *not* go any further, Lucifer!"

This cardinal was thick as a brick, and I was losing my patience.

Just then, Pope Julius II walked our way and approached us. "Excuse me," he said. "I overheard your dispute." Looking at the cardinal, he added, "Cardinal Mattone, it is clear that he has no eyes, but what about you? Can *you* not see?"

The cardinal swallowed hard, nervous. "I don't understand, Your Holiness. I can see clearly. This dirty snake is attempting to fool me, I mean *us*. You stand before the Devil, Pope Julius!"

The pope laughed as he put his arm around me. "This is Nostrildamus, Cardinal Mattone. He is a Frenchman and a seer, destined for great acclaim."

As I sighed with relief, the cardinal's shoulders drooped with embarrassment. With eyes like a scolded puppy, the cardinal said, "I'm sorry, Your Eminence. But may I ask, how do you know this sna—uh, seer?"

Pope Julius patted my back and stepped backward, as he replied, "I am the *Pope*. It is my business to know such things."

"Thank you," I said with a sigh. Boy was I glad the pope finally stifled this kooky cardinal's beak!

"My pleasure, Nostrildamus," the pope replied. Turning toward the cardinal, he added, "You may resume your business, Cardinal Mattone. I will escort our guest to the chapel."

The cardinal leaned over, kissed the pope's ring, and flew off, joining a flock of cardinals.

Julius grasped my hand. "Come!"

Danny's voice sounded, "That cardinal was a bird brain all right. But this is starting to get a little interesting, Nosy, and a bit freaky, especially since I spoke about Eve biting into the apple earlier today with Ms. Minnts."

"Well, Danny, this may be *my* story, but I am in *your* mind. So I imagine there will be some crossovers. Allow me to continue."

Chapter 4

$\mathcal{T}$he pope escorted me down a series of hallways, and we exited the huge basilica. We then walked a short distance to the quaint Sistine Chapel. The pope opened the huge wooden door and we entered the chamber.

The chapel was rather large, rectangular in shape, with a mosaic-tiled floor and a sixty-eight–foot-high ceiling. Consuming the entire space was a huge wooden scaffold, which the artist constructed in order to reach the ceiling to paint various scenes from the Bible.

Gazing up, the pope shook his head angrily. "What a crime!" he huffed.

I tried to focus my internal eye to see what the pope was referring to, but it was still hazy. Although I have no eyes, my mind creates a video-like version of reality, but often times it is not clear or it fades to black. And unfortunately, my mind's eye was seeing dark, grainy images. "Pope Julius," I said, "I can usually sense something, but I'm afraid I can't see a thing."

"Oh, my apologies," said the pope. "How rude of me. But this is one time that being blind is a godsend, Nostrildamus, because this ugly defilement of my sacred ceiling is not something anyone should see. It *must* be fixed."

I scratched my head, confused. "Why did your artist commit this crime? Is he a lunatic or vindictive?"

"Oh, dear me, no, no," he replied. "This sacrilegious mess was not made by the artist I commissioned, but rather by some deranged vandal. Someone splattered different colors of paint all over his masterpiece."

"Oh my, that's terrible," I said, as the pope continued, "Indeed it is! Allow me to escort you up the scaffolding. I'll introduce you to my master artist."

As we ascended the creaky wooden stairs, my mind's eye was getting clearer and clearer the closer we came to the frescoed ceiling. Taking the final step onto the highest plank, I saw beautifully painted figures of men, women, angels, and sibyls, yet splattered blobs of paint ruined them all. Just then a red blur grew larger and larger in my mind's eye, when I heard a body approaching, the pitter-patter of its feet rumbling the wooden floor planks.

"Who is this green snake!?" the figure bellowed to the pope as he pointed his paintbrush at my face like a dagger. "Is *he* the villain!?"

"No, no, not at all," Pope Julius said.

Meanwhile, my vision of this little red man had suddenly come into focus. I was taken aback! He was a large chunk of cherry jello supported by two little legs.

Despite his grumpiness, he was a cute little fella with a beard and mustache. And his cherry gelatin looked quite scrumptious, especially as it jiggled with each agitated gesture he made. I stifled a chuckle, as I said, "I came to see if I could be of any help."

He laughed. "To *see* if you can help!? Without eyes?" Turning toward the pope, he added in a huff, "If this was your idea, Your Holiness, to send a sightless jester to cheer me up, you've wasted your time. I'm in no mood for a farce!"

The pope kindly placed his hand on my shoulder. "Don't mind him, Nostrildamus. He is a moody artist, a bit grouchy at times." He then looked back at the irritated artist. "Nostrildamus happens to be a great seer from France. He does not need eyes to see what none of us are capable of seeing. So he can be of good use."

The artist's attitude softened, as he looked at me and bowed his head. "Excuse me. I didn't know you were a gifted seer, Nostrildamus. I will gladly accept any help you may provide."

I smiled. "That is quite all right. No offense taken. I will be happy to assist in anyway I can."

He lifted his head. "I am Michelanjello, the greatest artist in all of Italy."

The pope chuckled. "And Michelanjello is a bit modest, too."

Michelanjello's face twisted as he retorted, "Do you mock me, Your Eminence?"

Julius smiled. "You are indeed great, Michelanjello. Superlative, in fact. But all of Italy and beyond knows of another sublime soul

named Lionardo Da Vinci, your older rival. And a majestic lion Da Vinci is, for his marvelous inventions, curiosity, and diversity are unrivalled."

"Yes, yes, I know, I know," Michelanjello said crabbily as he pulled out a sketch he had made of Lionardo. "I keep him in my back pocket at all times, where he deserves to be, because Lionardo can kiss—"

"That's enough!" the pope commanded. "I know you two have a distaste for one another, but you are in the Lord's house, so rule your tongue."

Michelanjello gritted his teeth grumpily as his jello jaw jiggled. He gazed down at the sketch once more, then crumbled it and stuffed it back in his rear pocket. Humiliated, he looked back up at his illustrious ceiling that was cruelly marred, and griped, "Do you see this mess, Your Holiness? You forced me—a sculptor—to paint this ceiling, which robbed me of four years of my life, and now what? Do you expect me to strip and repaint everything all over again?"

Michelanjello glanced longingly at his unused set of chisels and mallets, then back at the pope. "I was born to chisel rough blocks of marble to release the magnificent figures trapped within, yet you task me with grinding minerals to make paint, which I then must apply to wet plaster before it dries." Spinning around, he pointed to all the figures he had drawn and painted. "Look at all these scenes I have created for Your Holiness. Destroyed, ruined! Just like my career and my life!"

I swallowed a lump of sympathy. I now understood why he was so crabby and miserable. I couldn't imagine spending four years of my life, first, sketching all these figures on paper, then building a scaffold to reach the ceiling, then transferring that sketch onto the ceiling, and finally working with wet plaster and paint, day after day, month after month, year after year to complete this colossal task. The neck strain alone (of having to look up as you paint) must have been painful enough, never mind the fact that Michelanjello loathed the paint brush, favoring a chisel instead.

I stepped closer. "Michelanjello," I said with compassion. "As I mentioned, I came here to help you. Can you think of anyone that would do such a terrible thing?"

Michelanjello's face twisted with disgust as he angrily rubbed his paintbrush clean with a dirty rag. "Well, there is only one fool who could possibly dislike me: Lionardo Da Vinci. That old buzzard had said some nasty things, like trying to compare *me*, the greatest sculptor in the world, to a silly baker, just because I'm often covered in white marble dust. Then he said my figures look like canvas bags filled with rocks!" Angrily, he threw the dirty rag onto the scaffold's wooden floorboards and stomped his foot. "Huh! The sheer nerve!"

"Listen, my son," Pope Julius said in a soft, fatherly tone. "There seems to be some merit to what Lionardo said. Your previous works contained figures that looked very natural in form, quite beautiful, like your statues of the *Pieta* and *David*. Yet as I had mentioned to you, this fresco is quite different. Some of your women look like men, with bulging muscles, such as your Cumaean Sibyl. Look at her. She looks like Hercules. Why this obsession with muscles and masculinity?"

Michelanjello huffed. "I know my anatomy well, Your Eminence. Yet let my expression of women be my own, not yours or anyone else's. I have my reasons."

The pope's shoulders dropped. He and Michelanjello butted heads quite often and he wasn't going to push this issue anymore. "Very well, I relent, because your remaining figures form an amazing masterpiece that will thrill the world and generations to come." He reached over and grasped Michelanjello's shoulder. "But

I must say, accusing Lionardo of defacing your work is unfounded. He is far too great of an artist to destroy your works with graffiti. His method has always been to simply create another masterpiece to rival or surpass yours."

I cleared my throat. "Hu-hum. Excuse me, but who else might be spiteful enough to do such a thing?"

They both looked at me and shrugged their shoulders. Michelanjello scratched his wiry beard, thinking, while the pope looked at the graffiti. "I don't know what else to say, Nostrildamus. I can't fathom someone doing such a vile thing, especially in a sacred chapel."

I nodded. "Yes, I agree, it's shameful. But perhaps if I concentrate hard enough, my visions will give us a clue as to whom this vandal might truly be."

The pope smiled and gazed at me. "That would be splendid, Nostrildamus."

Michelanjello shook his head as he glanced at his ruined fresco. "Even if you find the culprit, Nostrildamus, the damage has been done. It is beyond repair. Who will repaint this entire fresco? You?"

"I can't help you in that regard," I said. "My drawings look like a Wimpy Kid's stick figures."

Michelanjello and Pope Julius both squinted, confused.

I realized that the knowledge I gained from my time travel to the twenty-first century was lost on these Renaissance men. "Well, what I meant is that I cannot draw or paint as magnificently as you, so that's out of the question, but I will not give up."

The pope smiled with appreciation. "I know you are a great thinker, Nostrildamus. So please, have a seat and take your time. You have performed miraculous feats in the past, so we'll all pray you will do so again today."

Breaking the spell of my beautiful narration, Danny's voice sounded, "Hey, Nosy. This tale of yours has some familiar characters. I've heard of those two artists in class. But boy are they bizarre looking!"

I smiled. "Ms. Minnts will be pleased to hear that, Danny. But, yes, as I said, I guarantee this tale will be quite imaginative, so expect some variations of reality. After all, imagination *is* more important than knowledge."

"Oh, gees, you're not gonna hit me with that Einstein nonsense, are ya? Well, I ain't buying it, Nosy."

"Well, it's not mine to sell, it's Einstein's." As Danny moaned, I added, "But just hang in there, Danny. Only time will tell. Anyhow, it's good to know you've been paying attention, and even to *some* things in school."

"Well, your story *is* getting a bit more interesting, Nosy, so I guess I don't wanna wake up yet."

"Very well, slumber head, shall I continue?"

"Sure, let it rip."

Chapter 5

As Michelanjello and Julius strolled along the scaffolding, chatting solemnly, I clenched my hands into fists, straining to make this miracle come true. But the harder I tried the less I saw. As the smell dusty plaster filled my senses, the hungrier I got. Actually, it wasn't the plaster that titillated my senses; it was the savory scents of pasta, meatballs, and cappuccino that were wafting through the building. I felt totally ashamed of myself. How could I tell them I was hungry at a time like this, when they were both grieving about this horrible defacement of a masterpiece? No sooner did I think that, than my stomach let out this embarrassing, humongous growl!

Michelanjello and the pope pivoted toward me, as Julius declared, "Ah, how inconsiderate—"

My green skin turned red! I was utterly ashamed. I felt like slithering under a rock, when the pope continued, "I should have offered you something to eat first. Where are my manners?"

As I sighed with relief, Michelanjello vented, "Sacrifice! *I* sacrificed for four years to create this work. Yet you cannot wait four hours to eat?"

Julius grasped Michelanjello's arm. "Please, Nostrildamus has traveled not from around the corner, but from a distant place in the cosmos to help us. Certainly you can find it in your heart to allow him a meal."

Michelanjello threw his paintbrush on the floor and plopped down on a wooden crate, as his gelatin body bounced and rippled. "Very well!" he whined. "But I must insist that you have the food brought up here. I'm sure slithering down the scaffold stairs to the dining hall would only further upset his unruly stomach, which is getting louder and more irritating by the second!"

As Julius rolled his eyes, I said, "That's fine. You both are right. I do need to eat; yet the seriousness of this artistic dilemma does exceed our own needs. It is imperative that great art lives on forever, so we must do everything in our power to rectify this great injustice."

As both men smiled, appeased, and the pope called down below for a servant to get our food, I wiped the sweat off my forehead. *Whoa!* I thought. *Very good, Nostrildamus. You get an A+ in diplomacy!*

As we sat waiting for our food, Pope Julius scribbled some military notes in his journal, since he wished to forcefully reunite Italy, while Michelanjello sketched plans for Julius's colossal, marble memorial. Whether he was looking to glorify Julius for all eternity, or himself, by accomplishing such a grand feat, I don't know, but all I did know is that I was sitting between two powerful titans.

But in my mind, Michelanjello's cherry-red gelatin body was starting to look more and more appetizing as my starving stomach cried to eat. My tongue licked my lips, as I could almost taste how delicious that succulent jello would be.

Thank heavens our food arrived just in time. I hate to think what might have happened if four more hours had rolled by. I know many kids use the excuse *my dog ate my homework,* but if I had to say *I ate Michelanjello,* I don't think people or the history books would look too kindly on me.

Well, as I said, I love to eat, and the pasta, meatballs, and cappuccino were *fantastico!* I had picked up a few Italian words on my visit, too. Anyhow, as my belly relished the food, my mind rumbled with questions, and the most important one I had to ask again. "Michelanjello, a terrible vandalism like this was most likely done by someone who dislikes you very much. Are you sure there isn't someone out there that despises you?"

Michelanjello looked at me, surprised, as if the thought of someone not liking *him*, the greatest artist alive, was absurd. Except for Lionardo, naturally. But then his eyes widened. "Ah, yes, of course!" he said as he rubbed his nose with an irritable twitch. "How could I ever forget…it must be Pietro Torrigiano!"

I rose up on my tail, excited. "Who is that?" I implored.

Michelanjello's face twisted with disgust. "Pietro was a fellow student, back in the days when we studied in Florence together. I was seventeen, and that weasel couldn't accept the fact that I was a greater artist than he, so he hammered me a shot, right to the nose! This dent is a constant reminder of that filthy animal's anger and jealousy. Yes, yes," he said, as he patted his crooked nose. "Pietro would certainly have a motive to destroy my fresco!"

The pope walked over and nodded. "I do recall hearing about that incident many years ago." He gazed at me. "Perhaps that's something worth looking into…I mean—" the pope was clearly embarrassed, as he stumbled with his words, "uh, well, you can't really *look* at or into anything, now can you, but what I meant to say was—"

I smiled. "Yes, I know what you meant, Pope Julius. I will *investigate* this matter. This Pietro chap certainly has a motive worth examining." I turned toward Michelanjello. "Do you know where Pietro lives?"

He nodded and eagerly conveyed the directions. Not wishing to confront Pietro with his old enemy by my side, I told Michelanjello to stay put, while I investigate the matter.

Slithering down the scaffold with my trusty staff, I made my way out of the Vatican and scurried to Pietro's small apartment in the heart of the eternal city.

In my mind, a vision of Pietro appeared. I recoiled! He was working on a small clay model of a *funeral* monument. Eagerly, I knocked on the door with my staff.

Pietro opened the door and greeted me warmly enough. But with Michelanjello's fresco ruined and Pietro working on a funeral piece, I was now concerned that Pietro had more than graffiti on his mind. "Hello," I said, "I work at the royal court of the king of France. He is always on the lookout for talented artists, and I happened to see a vision of you working on that very fine clay model. Do you mind if I inspect it closer?"

After I explained my ability to see things in my mind, Pietro grinned, happy to be complimented on his artwork and at the idea of possibly gaining another commission. "By all means, please come in," he said.

Quickly, I slithered over to the clay model, leaned closer and ran my fingers across it to feel if Michelanjello's name was inscribed on it.

Yes, that may have been wishful thinking (hoping to immediately nab this vandal and prospective murderer), but deep down I knew he wouldn't be foolish enough to carve Michelanjello's name on it, at least not *yet!* So I asked, "From what I can feel and see in my mind, it is quite beautiful, Pietro, even unfinished." Then came the *killer* questions. "But why would you be sculpting a funeral piece? Has someone died, or do you expect someone to die *soon*?"

Pietro's eyes and lips twitched nervously, as he replied, "I'd r-rather not say," he stuttered.

I remained gracious, despite burning with suspicion. "Why not? Your work is exquisite."

His eyes shrank with embarrassment. "Well, it pains me to say this, but this funeral monument shall not be for anyone here in Italy. You see, I had fled my beloved homeland of Florence many years ago after an incident there. I had moved to England and just returned to Rome two days ago to examine the work of my peers so I can finalize my design. Then I shall head back to England. This funeral piece is for King Henry VII. He died three years ago."

I sighed. I was glad to hear that Pietro's death sculpture was *not* for Michelanjello. But that he had mysteriously fled Florence, and now needed to examine the work of his peers (or perhaps *destroy* the work of his peer), concerned me. "There's no need to be ashamed that your commission comes from England, Pietro. However, I must ask: What incident occurred in Florence that forced you to leave Italy?"

Pietro glanced at the floor uneasily, then back at me. "I don't care to talk about those days. We were young and, well, you see, I had a fight with, with a very famous artist."

Pietro was very reluctant, but after I buttered him up good, like a Butterball turkey, Pietro's whole tale rolled out of his mouth. And I must say, it differed *greatly* from Michelanjello's. I then found myself stuck between two sides of the same story, not knowing who was really telling the truth. I had hit a brick wall, at least for now. With a sigh, I thanked him for his time and headed back toward the Vatican.

Once again, Danny's voice sounded, "I don't know, Nosy, this Pietro character sounds pretty guilty to me."

I got up from my *caquetoire*—you remember, that silly French chair!—and I grasped an apple. Taking a bite, I replied, "One cannot jump to conclusions so quickly, Danny. Pietro had offered me a compelling argument, which you need to hear before passing judgment."

"I suppose so," Danny replied. "And now that you mention it, Michelanjello is a pretty feisty dude, too. Isn't he?"

"Indeed he is. So sit tight, Danny, and keep listening, because the plot thickens."

Chapter 6

Slithering into the Sistine Chapel and up the scaffolding, I reached the top, where Michelanjello and the pope were waiting impatiently. The pope inquired eagerly, "So, what did you find out? Is Pietro the vandal?"

I rubbed my lips. "Actually, Pietro's story was rather interesting." I faced Michelanjello. "He said that *you* often made sarcastic remarks to your fellow students in Florence, and at him in particular. He explained that while you were all learning how to draw in the Chapel of Masaccio, you had harshly ribbed him. And that's why he smashed you in the nose, causing your bone and cartilage to crack like a biscuit."

Michelanjello huffed grumpily. "That's what *he* and *some* people say." He rubbed his crooked nose. "But this dent and I say Pietro was the troublemaker! That's why he fled Florence to perform a few commissions here in Rome, and then abandoned Italy all together to serve the King of England. He's a bully *and* a runaway traitor. Isn't that proof enough?"

I exhaled briskly as I tapped the scaffold floorboards with my staff. "No! That's what *I* call conjecture. Those circumstances might appear to make Pietro look guilty, but it's a conclusion without hard evidence."

This case was *not* getting easier. Pietro had made a good point; At times, Michelanjello *could* be a grumpy goat with prickly horns that get under your skin. Was Michelanjello the sarcastic bully that got what he deserved? Then again, why did Pietro flee Florence? Running away from an incident certainly makes anyone look guilty.

Pope Julius looked at me, disappointed. "I guess that brings us to a dead end. What do we do now? Just clean up this mess and give up?"

"No!" I said. "Evidence *will* appear eventually."

Just then, a spark went off in my head upon hearing the words *clean up this mess.* I slithered over to the fresco and pressed my large, sensitive nose near the graffiti paint and took a deep whiff.

"Hmm, very interesting," I said. "I should have done this sooner. It appears this paint is some form of latex or acrylic."

Michelanjello and the pope looked at one another, confused by my last two strange words, then gazed back at me with curious eyes.

I scratched a small piece of graffiti paint off the fresco. I held it in one hand, then pulled on it with the other. It stretched! "Well, I can tell you one thing for sure, Michelanjello. This paint is *not* from this time period."

Excited, the brilliant artist scurried closer. "What do you mean? Are you saying this nasty vandal is from the future?"

"He just might be," I said. "This paint is not brittle like your tempera paint. You see, I have come across many different types of paint during my journeys to the future. Allow me a moment to concentrate. If I can hone in on any cosmic activity about artists and their paints, I will channel it into my mind's eye."

Pope Julius glanced heavenward. "Thank you, Lord, for bringing this miraculous seer to our aid."

I shook my finger sideways. "No, Your Holiness. I haven't performed any miracle, yet. But as I said, I will try."

"That is all we can ask," the pope replied.

My brain ignited, as faces of famous artists flashed through my mind, when, suddenly, the slideshow stopped! It landed on the famous Dutch painter Hippopotamus Bosch.

Yes, of course! I thought. Bosch's artwork *is* very evil and creepy looking, like his *Garden of Earthly Delights*. Anyone who painted such gruesome visions of Hell would certainly have a good reason to defile a religious work of art.

But after a moment or two, I realized the Hellish Hippo couldn't be the villain; Bosch lived in *that* time period. The criminal's paint was some form of latex, a substance not yet invented.

I glanced at the vision of Bosch's scary rendition of Hell one last time. Actually, I loved it. It *was* wild and weird, but pretty darn amazing.

I realized that during Bosch's lifetime he had experienced the plague, or Black Death. The disease had started almost two hundred years earlier, around 1346, but recurred many times at different places in Europe over the following centuries, killing millions of people. It was utterly terrifying. So Hippopotamus Bosch was not evil, he was just expressing in art the horrible fear of death that so many people felt at that time, and he did it magnificently.

Meanwhile, Julius and Michelanjello had returned to their tasks, the pope nibbling on biscotti and devising strategies to expand the church, while Michelanjello continued designing the colossal monument to glorify Orange Julius.

Okay, I apologize! I'm getting parched and could use a cold drink, but, fine, scratch that.

Humiliated, I sat on a crate, slapping my tail against the wooden scaffold, trying to figure out who the villain might be. My mind turned and burned feverishly, but I was getting overwhelmed. There have been hundreds of famous artists over the years, so finding the culprit was like trying to find a grain of sugar in a large cake. My mind churned image after image, scanning faces and artwork as I advanced slowly toward the future. Once more, the slideshow stopped, this time landing on Carrotvaggio.

Hmm, I love carrots, too! Carrot cake is *really* tasty. It's also good with…oh, okay, okay, I'm sorry; I must focus.

But seriously, Carrotvaggio was a truly gifted artist. His dramatic use of chiaroscuro (which is the use of light and shadow to make images appear more three dimensional and realistic) and his unique compositions (which displayed figures in awkward positions) had influenced many others, like Ruebens and Rumbrand, which also happen to be my favorite sandwich and a pirate's favorite liquor, regardless of brand.

But despite Carrotvaggio's genius, he was also a ruffian, a gambler, and a fighter who even murdered a man in a brawl. Perhaps *he* was the…na! Again, wrong time period. Carrotvaggio lived from 1571 to 1610. Latex paint was invented much later.

Putting my mind into high gear, the images zoomed past the baroque, rococo, and impressionist eras and into the twentieth century of cubism, surrealism, and abstraction.

Ah, yes, I thought, *much, much better.* There were plenty culprits in this time period to consider. And with their radical breaks from tradition, I imagined quite a few of them would have a very good motive to destroy the past. After all, with a name like Andy Warhall, I'm sure he'd love to stroll down the hall of time to declare war on the past.

Quickly, I turned toward Michelanjello. "I think it would be best if you and I take a trip into the future. I have several good leads and suspects I'd like to investigate."

The pope placed his journal down and nodded. "Yes, you must go, Michelanjello. Perhaps this vandal could tell us what type of paint he used. It may be something that could be removed without damaging your artwork."

Michelanjello's eyes lit up as he dropped his pencil and folded up his sketch of the memorial. "That would be wonderful! It would save me another four years of my life, time I could devote to your memorial and getting back to what I do best—sculpture."

It was good to see Michelanjello smile for once. I must admit, previously, I was hesitant to even respond to Michelanjello, fearing the angry chunk of jello would flare up like the Incredible Hulk, or turn into the Thing, his jello hardening into rock. But now his whole attitude seemed to change, from a grumpy little grouch into a joyful jug of gelatin. Things were looking up.

Danny's voice sounded, "They certainly are, Nosy! This tale is better than I thought. I'm glad you entered my head."

"Well, that's splendid news, Danny. But there's still plenty more to come. So brace yourself; it's time for another time warp!"

Chapter 7

Excitedly, we both dashed out of the chapel, over the Tiber River, and plowed through the crowds of people strolling along the Via Veneto. Having located the alley where the invisible T-Zap was parked, we waited for the coast to be clear. I then flipped the switch on my staff to materialize the machine, and we hopped in. Quickly, I set the date to August 11, 1956 and then typed in *"Portlligat*, Catalonia, Spain."

Michelanjello tapped my arm. "Why August 11, and Spain?"

"Well, the August date mysteriously popped into my head, but I think we can kill two birds with one stone in Spain. I don't mean literally kill them, but you'll see what I mean."

I pulled the lever, and with a boom and a puff, the T-Zap zapped us through the mystical corridor of time, landing in a deserted field in Catalonia Spain. The view was quite pretty, with grassy hills, jagged mountains near the sea, and plenty of small boats, either sailing along or beached peacefully on the shoreline.

I looked around. "Perfect! No people. No explanations. Let's go!"

Michelanjello and I jumped out and I turned the cloaking device on. As we headed toward the seaside village of *Portlligat*, Michelanjello asked, "Who are we going to see?"

"Another genius, like you. Except his works are very strange and surreal. His name is Salvador Dolly. Yet he likes to be called Matador Dolly. You know, being Spanish and all."

"I hope that's not a lot of *bull*?" Michelanjello jested with a smile.

I laughed. "No, but the Matador *will* slay you with his astounding artwork."

As we strolled through the grassy field and onto a cobble-stoned street, I added, "Many of his works appear to be crazy dreams, yet most have subtle or hidden meanings."

"Well, if this Matador Dolly is so crazy, do you think he might be the vandal?"

"I doubt it," I said. "Dolly has painted a number of religious paintings, being a devout

Catholic. So I can't imagine him defacing a religious work of art such as yours."

Strolling into the village, I asked a woman where the artist lived, and she gave us directions. As I slithered up the path, and Michelanjello walked beside me, we came to the front door. With my staff, I knocked!

A few moments later, Dolly's wife, Gala, opened the door. "Greetings," she said. "May I help you?"

"Yes," I said. "My name is Nostrildamus and this is Michelanjello. We would like to see—"

"Oh my!" Gala exclaimed with joy. "Please come in, my husband will be delighted to see you. But how on earth did you ever manage to defy time and space?"

As she escorted us to Dolly's studio, I explained my fortunate meeting with O.G. Swells and so on. No sooner did we arrive, did Dolly spin around on his chair in front of his easel and say, "My, my! What a cosmic surprise for my dreamy eyes!"

As we approached him, I was going to break out into song, singing "Hello Dolly," but instead said, "I imagine you would also like an explanation as to how we got here. Yes?"

"No, no. That won't be necessary," Dolly said as he stood up and pointed to his painting with his doll-like arm, complete with rivets at the joints. "Allow me to explain why. This is *Nature Morte Vivante*, or in English, *Living Sill Life*."

Michelanjello recoiled. "Your still life is *not* still!" He scratched his head. "I have painted the Lord flying through space, which can be easily imagined. But lifeless objects floating and flying is pure madness."

"I believe you mean pure genius!" Dolly said as he stood proudly erect. With a smile, he then twisted the tip of his pointy moustache with his doll-like, plastic fingers.

Michelanjello looked at me, pointed his index finger at his brain and spun it in a circular motion. "I believe in Spanish he is called *loco!*"

As I chuckled, Dolly ignored the insult and explained, "Michelanjello, I live in a nuclear age. Things you could never have even dreamed of in your time have come to be. Art, physics, and science, which I call Nuclear Mysticism, are all merged in this painting. This mysticism also explains how you both traversed the mystical dimensions of time. And *that* is why I didn't need an explanation; the great Dolly knows *how* you got here." He straightened out his matador suit and hat, and added, "So the real question is: *why* did you come here?"

Michelanjello's head lowered as he replied solemnly, "Someone has destroyed my ceiling fresco in the Sistine Chapel. Different colors of paint now blot out my masterpiece."

I added, "But the paint is not tempera or oils, Dolly, it appears to be a modern substance. That's why I offered to assist Michelanjello in finding the culprit here, in your time period."

Dolly's plastic face reddened with irritation as his eyes widened. "You don't suspect that *I* had anything to do with it, do you?"

"Of course not," I said, "But—"

"Indeed not!" Dolly interjected. "Come with me," he added, as he strut toward a huge canvas. It was covered with a red-velvet cloth, which he yanked away swiftly, like a matador. He then pointed at his surreal rendition of the Crucifixion. "This is called *Corpus Hypercubus.* It is one of many of my contributions to the grand tradition of Roman Catholic art." He turned back to look at Michelanjello, and added, "Your art has inspired me, as it has millions of others. I would *never* destroy something so magnificent as your fresco in the Sistine Chapel." Dolly's insulted, theatrical face was all-aglow with sincerity as his piercing eyes bore holes into us.

I got the message, loud and clear, while Michelanjello replied, "My apologies, *signore* Dolly. I do believe you." He glanced back up at the strikingly bizarre painting, which was rendered in greater technical detail than even Michelanjello could muster. He was truly impressed, but also puzzled, as he said, "Its execution is marvelous, Dolly, but why is your Christ a giant, and not even nailed to that floating three-dimensional cross?"

Dolly spun around and pointed to the cubes that formed the cross. "It is not three-dimensional, Michelanjello, it is a Tesseract, *four*-dimensional. These advanced mysteries have inspired new meaning in this nuclear age of mine. Just as the four-dimensional hypercube baffles us mortals, so too does God's existence, hence being most fitting for this ultimate of mysteries." He then gazed at the small blocks floating in front of Christ's body with his piercing eyes. "Jesus appears to be floating, yet he also appears to be nailed by those four floating cubes—a visual illusion that adds to the mystery of the Holy Trinity." Then gazing down at Mary, he concluded, "As for Christ's gargantuan size in contrast to Mary, is not God colossal in comparison to all mankind?"

Michelanjello paused in thought for but a moment, when he smiled. "Indeed he is. And quite oddly, I'm beginning to see your not-so-crazy logic."

I stepped forward, eager to move our investigation along. "So, Dolly, can you think of an artist that uses latex-based paint?"

Dolly turned toward me, twisting his mustache, thinking. "Hmm, let me see. With latex and acrylic paints nowadays, there are many artists experimenting with these new mediums."

He began pacing back and forth with his doll-like, robotic walk, when I asked, "Do you think Pablo Pickaxo would know?" Pablo being the other bird I wished to kill, uh, contact, with one stone.

Dolly stopped. "Ah, my fellow Spaniard. Perhaps. Let me give him a call. Give me a minute. Do excuse me," he said, as he scurried over to his wacky lobster telephone, which sat on the far side of the studio.

Meanwhile, in my mind I noticed a book about Pickaxo on Dolly's desk and invited Michelanjello over to see how art had progressed. Opening the book, he saw a photo of Pablo standing by one of his paintings.

Michelanjello's eyes buggered out of his head like two small jack-in-the-boxes. "Dear God!" he cried. "What sort of madness is this?"

As I smiled, he continued, "At first I thought Dolly was mad, but his explanations and technical expertise undoubtedly confirm he is a genius. But as for *this* childish drivel, it is pure poppycock." His gelatin gut jiggled with indigestion as he gazed at Pickaxo's *Woman in Hat and Fur Collar*. "She has a flat face with two eyes on one side of her head, like him."

Michelanjello shook his head, disappointed and baffled. "They seem to be looking sideways, but also straight at us. Most peculiar."

"I guess it's all about seeing differently," I said. As he flipped another page, I added, "Believe it or not, Pablo Pickaxo is considered the new Michelanjello by some people."

Michelanjello's face reddened even more than his natural cherry-flavored color, as he grumbled, "That's an insult! They should take a pickax to Pickaxo's paintings. They call this progress? Huh! This is primitive. Progress has moved backwards. I have seen children in my day draw with more skill."

Just then, Dolly returned with a grin on his plastic face. "I spoke to Pablo, and he made a very good suggestion."

Michelanjello huffed. "I doubt such an amateur could ever make a good suggestion." He glanced down at the photo of Pablo and his artwork and pointed at it. "My suggestion to this crazy ax is *throw out your trash!* No sense in littering civilization with junk."

Dolly cleared his throat. "Well, you are not alone with your opinion, Michelanjello. But many others regard him with the highest praise. Pablo simply thinks differently and sees things from various perspectives. So although his technical skills may not have advanced past yours and your Renaissance peers, his mind has sought new avenues of expression." As Michelanjello twisted his lips, not buying the Matador's explanation, Dolly continued, "Yet, if you think *his* work is insane, then I'm sure you'll find his suggestion to be even more radical."

Michelanjello snickered. "What artist could possibly be more radical than Pickaxo?"

Dolly smiled. "The artist is an American, named Jackson Polyp."

"Polyp!? He sounds like an unwanted growth to me," Michelanjello quipped.

Dolly and I chuckled, realizing the Renaissance master could not appreciate or understand most modern art. That would be like expecting us to understand how a Xenotronic Discombilitator from the year 3025 works. Actually, I do know how it works, I've visited the future; remember? Okay, bad example, but nevertheless, Dolly pulled out a book on Jackson Polyp's artwork. As he opened it, Michelanjello choked! "You must be jesting!? Your world has truly gone mad."

As he gazed at the photos of Polyp's work, he grasped the book and pulled it closer. "But, by Jesus, these splattered drips of paint look exactly like those that sullied my fresco. This artless polyp *must* be the culprit!"

Quickly, I slithered over and peered down at the book, summoning my mind to see the vision of Polyp's artwork and scan his biography. I was tongue-tied. After a moment or two, I said, "I have to agree. This must be our man!"

We both thanked Dolly and made a beeline back to the T-Zap.

Danny's voice boomed excitedly, "Oh, this Polyp dude is the man all right, Nosy. Hurry up! I'm dying to hear the rest of this."

I smiled. "Okay, okay, I moving..."

Chapter 8

$\mathcal{H}$aving hopped into the T-Zap, I left the date set to August 11, 1956, but typed in Springs, Long Island, NY. I then pulled the lever. Off we went, with a boom, puff, and a cosmic zap!

Arriving in the quaint hamlet of Springs, in East Hampton, we then made our way to Polyp's small studio, which was essentially a tiny shack with cedar shingles.

Michelanjello snickered. "Huh! A suitable shack for a whacky hack."

I shook my head with a smile, pondering why Pietro had popped Michelanjello in the nose. I knocked on the door. But there was no answer.

Michelanjello stood on his tiptoes and peered in one of the windows. "This is Polyp's rat hole all right. The man doesn't even use an easel; he has a large canvas thrown on the floor with paint splattered all over it. But there's no sign of the Master *Mauler*."

No sooner did I giggle at Michelanjello's grumpy sarcasm, than a neighbor walking her prissy dog spotted us. The woman, wearing a classy Emilio Schuberth satin & fox trim dress, walked over, as her pompous white poodle with pompoms took a leak on the lawn. "I'm sorry," she said, "if you two are looking for Jackson Polyp, you're too late. He went for a ride in his Oldsmobile with two ladies. Knowing him, there's no telling when or *if* he'll be back."

Michelanjello and I sighed with disappointment. It looked like our investigation hit a dead end.

Meanwhile, her fancy fur-ball decided to do number two, pinching a Yodel on the lawn. It then lifted its snooty nose and tore up the grass with its hind legs, attempting to cover it.

Nice try, Fluffy, I thought, *but you didn't cover up your sins too well, just like this Jackson Polyp pup!*

The poodle finally finished doing its business, and then began sniffing Michelanjello's cherry-flavored butt. This made me nervous; I didn't want this prissy show dog taking a bite of my jell—uh, friend. Okay, relax; that was an honest slip!

Fortunately, the woman yanked her pooping poodle away, then asked, "What did you want to see Jackson about?"

Discreetly, I nudged the poodle further away with my staff as I said, "Well, I was just curious to know what kind of paint he uses."

"I wouldn't know," she said. Meanwhile, the wind began to moan and gray clouds eerily rolled in. "But I bet his apprentice knows. He's across the street in that barn." She pointed to a large, dilapidated structure that sat on a small hill. It looked like a haunted old house, half rotted with peeling paint and a sagging roof. Despite how creepy it looked, I was excited.

"Thank you," I said, as I grasped Michelanjello's hand.

As we scurried across the street, a nasty thunderclap let loose while drizzle speckled the pavement. In my mind's eye, I noticed the droplets of rainwater on the street, but also a faint trail of tiny paint drops, which led from Polyp's studio, straight across the street, and up the weed-infested lawn to the rickety old barn.

Just as we arrived, the apprentice unexpectedly walked out the door. Coming face-to-face with us, he recoiled with surprise. "Dear God!" he cried. "How did *you* get here?"

"You know us?" I asked, equally surprised.

"Y-yes," he stammered. "Of course, who doesn't know Michelanjello and Nostrildamus?"

"Well," I said. "Everyone knows of Michelanjello, but not everyone knows me. So how is it *you* do?" I rubbed my chin. "And why are you so flustered?"

The apprentice swallowed hard. "I like to r-read, Nostrildamus, that's how I know you. I've read your quatrains. Your predictions are quite astonishing." As we all shifted under an awning, out of the rain, he continued, "And naturally I'm a bit nervous, it's not every day I b-bump into famous people from the past. This *is* pretty amazing," he said with an excited grin.

I quickly mellowed to the teen's valid reasons as Michelanjello asked impatiently, "See here, son, I need to know what kind of paint your sloppy drip master uses?"

The apprentice's expression turned defensive, not appreciating the *sloppy drip* insult about his master. "All kinds. Why do you ask?"

"We're simply curious," I replied as I wiped the raindrops off my arms. "Do you have a key to Polyp's studio? I'd like to sample your master's paint."

The apprentice thought for a moment, then dug into his pocket to retrieve the key. "I'm not supposed to allow anyone to enter Jackson's studio, but since you're both important people, I guess I can make an exception."

Thunder suddenly roared, as black clouds twisted, looking like a Van Gogh painting. The apprentice eagerly locked the barn door, then walked us back to the studio through the rain. As we entered, Michelanjello walked over to the large canvas on the floor, while the apprentice inquired, "I still don't understand. Its just plain old paint. What are you looking for?"

Michelanjello's surveying eyes veered from the canvas up to the apprentice. "This is *not* plain *old* paint, son. It is very *new* paint. And it may very well be latex, which I believe Nostrildamus calls it."

"Yes," I said, "it might be. And I also noticed a trail of paint drips leading across the street to your barn."

The apprentice laughed. "You're blind, how could you see anything?" He pivoted and gazed out the window. "I don't see any paint drips."

Michelanjello rolled his eyes as he placed his hands on his hips. "Evidently, dear boy, the rain washed it away. But there *was* a trail."

"Oh, yes!" the apprentice said. "Mr. Warhall had stopped by the other day and stored a few cans of paint in my barn. One of the cans had a loose lid, so perhaps some paint *did* spill out."

Michelanjello's eyes widened. "Yes! Of course!" he exclaimed, as he glanced at me, then back at the teen. "This Andy Warhall fellow. Where is he now?"

"He lives in Manhattan, it's only about two hours from here."

Michelanjello raced toward the door, stopped, and pivoted around, his eyes fixed in my direction. "Let's go, Nostrildamus! He's the crazy devil you had first mentioned. He's the villain!"

The apprentice looked at us somewhat confused, but then nodded. "Well, if something crazy happened, I'll bet he's your man all right. Andy Warhall *is* a strange dude."

I slithered toward the door, and said, "Hold your horses, Michelanjello. Yes, I had mentioned Warhall first, but his artwork is not done with splattered drips. If there were Campbell's soup cans printed all over the place, perhaps, but let's not jump ahead of ourselves."

"Jumping, shlumping!" Michelanjello huffed. "That Warhall menace borrowed Polyp's paint to wage war on *me*, while making it look as if Polyp was the culprit. Very clever, but that warring warlock can't fool me. Now, shake a leg. Let's go!"

"Tut, tut!" I said. "First of all, I don't even have a leg to shake. Second, that's not how I conduct an investigation. I'll need to verify the evidence first." Slithering near the canvas on the floor, I leaned over and scooped up a smidgeon of wet paint with my index finger. Taking a sniff, I said, "Ah, yes indeed, very familiar."

The apprentice gazed at me. "What do you mean, familiar?"

Meanwhile, lightning flashed outside as pellets of rain smacked the windowpanes.

I wiped my finger on a rag, as I responded, "Having no eyes has made my other senses more acute. I can taste a mere gram of parsley in a meatball, or a pinch of thyme in a vat of tomato sauce. More importantly, my large aquiline nose is very adept at smelling. And this paint contains a synthetic that is exactly the kind used to vandalize Michelanjello's masterpiece."

The apprentice suddenly regarded me with suspicion, as he retorted, "Are you saying Mr. Polyp destroyed Michelanjello's fresco in the Sistine Chapel?"

I smiled. "No!" I said. "YOU did!"

The apprentice's eyes bulged with surprise as his face turned white. His head snapped left and right, then without warning, he darted for the door!

Quickly, I slithered after him and tackled him to the floor. We fell onto Polyp's wet canvas as he squirmed to get free. Floundering, like a tie-dyed fish, the apprentice was covered in a spectrum of bold colors.

Still holding him tight, I said, "Your attempt to flee only adds to sealing this case shut. So, I thank you. You're a pretty good liar, buddy boy, but *you're* the vandal of the Sistine scandal!"

As thunder and rain continued to rumble and roar outside, Michelanjello squinted with shock and confusion. "I don't get it. First I thought Polyp was our man, then Warhall." Gazing at the apprentice, he added, "And how, pray tell, did his running away help you arrive at that conclusion?"

The apprentice growled, "Michelanjello is right. Just because I ran doesn't mean I'm guilty."

As I struggled to maintain my grip on the slippery scoundrel, I said, "You fell into my verbal trap, you naughty boy. All I said was: Michelanjello's masterpiece was vandalized. I never mentioned *which* masterpiece. Yet you knew it was his fresco in the Sistine Chapel. That's why you ran and why you're guilty! And I'll bet there's a time machine hidden in your barn, which you so eagerly locked."

The apprentice frowned and stopped squirming, giving in to his crime.

We transported him back to the Sistine Chapel in 1512, and with his special paint remover and rags, he worked day and night to strip the graffiti off of Michelanjello's masterpiece. Charged with vandalism, he confessed that he despised the so-called masterpieces of the past, claiming that his master, Jackson Polyp, was the greatest artist of all time, and that his works should literally supplant those of the old masters. Having read O.G. Swells novel, *The Time Machine*, he, too, had built a transporter to complete his mission. He was charged a hefty fine and sentenced to serve six months in prison.

Meanwhile, Michelanjello restored the fresco back to its original splendor within two weeks. Afterward, an elated Pope Julius and Michelanjello hugged me and thanked me for solving the case. It was a joyous day as hundreds of people came to see the amazing masterpiece, their hearts and souls filled with admiration and awe. Michelanjello was a jolly-jello-fellow from that day on.

So you see, it's rewarding to help others in need, even if they're grumpy, and also wise to read, as knowledge opens new doorways to miraculous places.

Chapter 9

Danny woke up on the couch. He blinked hard and rubbed his eyes. Gazing up at the clock, he saw that it was only 4:40. The past twenty minutes had felt like two hours.

He leapt to his feet. "Gees! What the heck was that?"

He reached into his backpack and pulled out his art textbook. He thumbed through the pages, stopping at Leonardo and Michelangelo, then on to Hieronymus Bosch to admire his bizarre *Garden of Earthly Delights*. Then he turned to Caravaggio, and on again to Rubens and Rembrandt. He studied Rembrandt's portrait of *Aristotle*, then flipped back to compare it with Caravaggio's *Crucifixion of St. Peter*, noticing how Rembrandt had indeed learned from Caravaggio the technique of chiaroscuro. He then flipped ahead to the works of Salvador Dali, noticing how *he* had learned from Bosch. Navigating to the works of Pablo Picasso, he once again noticed how *he* had learned from Georges Braque.

Danny smiled as he recalled Ms. Minnts's words: *Ideas can't be hatched in a vacuum.*

As he closed the book he saw a small reproduction of Salvador Dali's surreal artwork, entitled *Sleep,* on the back cover. Danny squinted and drew the book closer. He shook his head as his mind reeled; *this weird* thing *looks a little like Nostrildamus.* He scratched his head. *Did I create Nosy subconsciously somehow, having only glanced at this back cover one day? Gees, ideas really do come from the least likely of places.*

His eyes then caught a glimpse of the bowl of raw carrots sitting on the kitchen table. But before Danny could even smile, his eyes sprang open wide as another thought flashed into his mind. *Gees, Nostrildamus said it pays to read, and boy was he right!*

Danny grasped a sticky note pad and jotted down: Study art book & tell Ms. Minnts she was right—imagination *is* more important.

Just then, another thought struck him, this one quite hard! *Oh, my, Nostrildamus also said…* Danny bolted into the garage, pulled his bike off the wall rack, and tore off down the street.

Up ahead, he saw Johnny, gloomily hunched over his bike, still trying to repair his flat tire. Danny raced up and came to a skid, stopping right in front of him.

Johnny looked up, surprised and confused, as he gazed at the box in Danny's hand. "Is that tube for me?" he asked, not sure if Danny was pulling a prank or being serious.

"It sure is, Johnny," Danny said as he hopped off his bike. "Here, let me help you."

Johnny stepped back, quasi stunned, as Danny pulled out his wrenches and screwdriver and began fixing his bike.

"Thanks, D-Danny," Johnny mumbled with a slight stutter. "I really appreciate this."

Danny glanced up and winked. "My pleasure, pal." Turning the last nut tight, and flipping the bike right side up, he added, "You're all set. It's as good as new."

Johnny smiled reluctantly. "Does this mean we're b-buddies?" he stuttered.

"Johnny, we've known each other for what?...thirteen or fourteen years? I think it's time we stop being stupid grumpy enemies."

"Sounds good to me, Danny."

Danny hopped on his bike. "But that doesn't mean I'll let you win a race!" With that, Danny popped a wheelie and started pedaling. "I'll race ya to the train station!"

Johnny hopped on his bike and tore off after Danny, shouting, "You have a head start, cheater!"

Danny applied his brakes until Johnny was at his side, then they both pumped like fiery steam engines toward the railroad station. Reaching the station first, and coming to a skidding halt, Danny raised his hands. "Whoa!"

Johnny pulled up close behind. "You won that fair and square, Danny. It must be that new bike of yours. She's a beauty."

"Would you like to try it?"

Johnny's eyes widened. "Are you kidding? Hell yeah!"

Exchanging bikes, Johnny glanced at Danny and smiled. "Race ya home!"

With that, Johnny tore off as Danny followed suit. But in the distance, Danny spotted the street workers he had seen earlier, each swinging their pickaxes, which he now saw in a strikingly different way.

Danny shook his head and resumed pedaling, yet as he passed the train station, he suddenly noticed the poster for the Bronx Zoo. Oddly enough, it featured a majestic lion and a hippopotamus.

Danny laughed as he happily followed his new buddy home, his mind percolating with new knowledge *and* imagination.

The End

Characters

Nostrildamus — **Nostradamus**
1503 – 1566

Nostradamus was a French physician and seer who published thousands of predictions in several volumes that have become world famous. Attracting the admiration of Queen Catherine de Medici, Nostradamus served in her court as a seer and physician for her son, the young King Charles IX of France.

O.G. Swells — **H.G. Wells**
1866 – 1946

Herbert George Wells was an English writer, and often cited as the father of sci-fi along with French author Jules Verne. Wells was light years ahead of most authors, and his visions have influenced countless authors, artists, and even scientists.

Michelanjello — **Michelangelo**
1475 – 1564

Michelangelo was an Italian sculptor, painter, architect and poet. However, he viewed himself, first and foremost, as a sculptor. Nevertheless, he was ordered by Pope Julius II to paint the Sistine Chapel's ceiling and later the altar wall. Although known to be strong-willed and moody, Michelangelo inevitably buckled under Pope Julius's iron fist. His art stands as the pinnacle of Renaissance art, along with Leonardo's.

Lionardo Da Vinci — **Leonardo Da Vinci**
1452 – 1519

Leonardo was an Italian polymath who excelled at every field of endeavor he engaged in, including painting, sculpture, architecture, mathematics, inventions, weaponry, botany, cartography, music and more. Leonardo was indeed the lion of his age, being the unrivalled king of intellectual curiosity and perhaps the world's most multi-faceted man. In the art world he is most noted for the *Mona Lisa* and *The Last Supper*.

Hippopotamus Bosch — **Hieronymus Bosch**
1450 -1516
A Dutch painter whose religious works are praised more so for their dark visions of Hell than those of Paradise. Bosch was a master visionary, centuries ahead of the surrealist movement made famous by Salvador Dali.

Pope Julius II
1443-1513

Born Giuliano della Rovere, Giuliano rose to become Pope Julius II in 1503. Nicknamed "The Warrior Pope" by some, Julius sought to unite Italy and enlarge the administrative capacity of the Roman Catholic Church. He ordered the demolition of the original St. Peter's Basilica, hiring Bramante and others to design and build the edifice that stands today. Julius commissioned Michelangelo to paint the ceiling and altar of the Sistine Chapel and later hired him to design the dome of the basilica itself, thus crowning a miraculous lifetime achievement, which although caused discord about its expense yielded a masterpiece in architecture and art.

Carrotvaggio — **Caravaggio**
1571-1610

Michelangelo Merisi de Caravaggio was an Italian painter whose dramatic and emotional use of lighting greatly influenced the Baroque era. His extreme talent was matched by his volatile temper, which landed him in jail numerous times. He was involved in a brawl and killed the man, yet whether it was self-defense or not was never revealed. His artworks, however, need no defense, as they stand on their own as inspiring masterworks.

Reubens — **Peter Paul Rubens**
1577-1640

Rubens was a Flemish Baroque painter whose works are noted for their action and sensuous full-figured women. His technique of painting flesh was masterful as was his ability to capture movement to tell a gripping story.

Rumbrand — **Rembrandt van Rijn**
1606-1669

Rembrandt was a Dutch painter and etcher whose works are often dark and bathed in a single light source. Heavily influenced by Caravaggio, Rembrandt's works became famous for their chiaroscuro, more so than his predecessor's, yet that assessment has changed in recent years, realizing Caravaggio's earlier precedent. However, Rembrandt's paintings are markedly different in that his works are more sedate, while Caravaggio often created dramatic compositions that were more complex and full of action. Rembrandt was a masterful painter at an early age, as his stunning portrait of *Nicolaes Ruts* attests, and his portraits remain golden gems of the genre.

Matador Dolly — **Salvador Dali**
1904-1989

Dali was a Spanish artist who helped establish surrealism, becoming its ultimate master. He was a painter, sculptor, photographer, and worked on films, animations, and in fashion. Shunned by some in the world of modern art for his technical prowess, his surrealism has been far more influential than cubism, abstraction and other genres in the advertising and entertainment worlds, having a massive impact far beyond what he is given credit for.

Pablo Pickaxo — **Pablo Picasso**
1881-1973

Picasso was a Spanish artist who co-invented cubism along with Georges Braque, and also worked with ceramics, printmaking, and sculpture. He is regarded by some as one of the greatest artists of the twentieth century.

Andy Warhall — **Andy Warhol**
1928-1987

Warhol was an American artist who began in the advertising field. His use of silk-screening quickly became in vogue, thus paving the way for his pop art and flamboyant fame.

Jackson Polyp — **Jackson Pollock**
1912-1956

Pollock was an American painter who trained under Thomas Hart Benton, yet broke free from all forms of realism entering into abstraction and becoming a leader of abstract expressionism. His drip paintings became his legacy after dying in a car accident on August 11, 1956, driving an Oldsmobile with two women.

Thank You

FOR READING
THIS *ARTISTIC* FANTASY!

If you enjoyed it, please take a second to post a brief review on your favorite retailer's or social media's website, such as Amazon.com, Barnes and Noble, Kobo, Goodreads.com etc.

Afterward, email us at info@dvbooks.net with the link to your review to receive a
FREE gift!
And a **discount** for *Meet My Famous Friends,* a cool picture book that features some of these same weird characters, like Michelanjello, Lionardo, and others, like Thomas Edisun, Susan Bee Anthony, Virginia Wolf, Albert Eine-Stein and more!

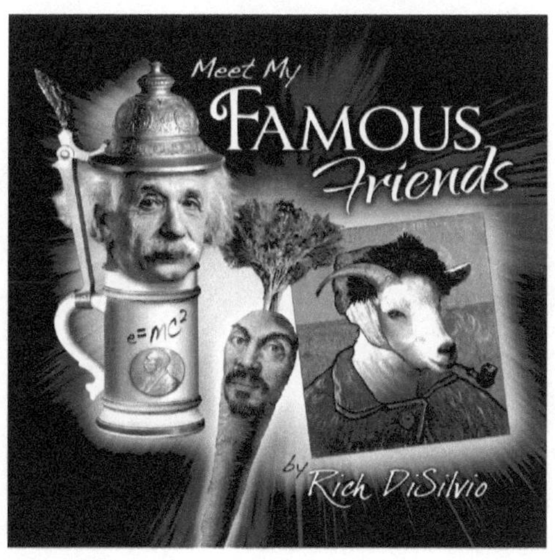